W9-AXN-232

PAWS FOR PASTA

MAUREEN MELVIN

Illustrated by Geoff Crook

CHAPMANS

Also by Maureen Melvin
with illustrations by Geoff Crook

PAWS FOR THOUGHT
PAWS AGAIN

For Nick, Charlie and Andrew

Ecco! une grande surprise pour vous.
I speaka French, Italian too.
Voilà, mes braves, c'est fini – basta,
Mon livre de cuisine, *Paws for Pasta!*

Chapmans Publishers Ltd
141-143 Drury Lane
London WC2B 5TB

A CIP Catalogue record for this book is available from the British Library

ISBN 1-85592-629-6

First published by Chapmans 1992

Designed by Judy Linard

Typeset by Monoset Typesetters

Printed and bound in Great Britain by
Butler & Tanner Ltd, Frome and London

Author's Note

All creatures like to eat and drink,
From man to mouse or mog.
But no one likes it more than me,
A gastronomic dog.

I had a mind to conjure up
A cookbook, all in rhyme.
I'd learn a little French, en route,
To add from time to time.

I took my scheme to Mummy,
Whom I thought it would enchant.
'A cookery book in verse?' she said,
'Oh, Abigail, you can't!'

'Oh yes, I can; just wait and see,'
I said, 'There's nothing to it!'
My brain went into overdrive,
I knew that I could do it.

And after many failures, flops,
Burnt offerings and worse –
I lined up all my favourite things
And coaxed them into verse.

Pointers

To every dog who likes to cook
And share the kitchen chores,
Remember not to overlook
A pair of well-scrubbed paws.

Before you start, line up your tools
And stand them in a row.
It's *de rigueur* in cooking schools,
No wandering to and fro.

Poised on your stool, the cordon bleu,
And stirring this and that,
No hairs, please, in the pot-au-feu;
Be sure to wear your hat.

If boeuf en croûte is on the go
And forepaws are required,
Wear rubber gloves, be *comme il faut*,
Exquisitely attired.

Staple Diet

My staple diet is rather nice –
Each day, two tablespoons of rice.
I like it brown but white will do,
Whatever seems the best for you.
I used to have a biscuit meal
But now and then I didn't feel
Too well, and Mr Griffin said
I ought to change to rice instead.
It soothes the tummyache away
And keeps cholesterol at bay.

And with the rice, to fill my dish,
A choice of poultry, meat or fish,
Or hard-boiled egg, a lovely treat.
And sometimes I have Shredded Wheat
If Mummy fails to cook the rice
In time for lunch; and once or twice
She hasn't even bought the stuff,
Which puts me in a dreadful huff.
I try to heed the vet's advice:
'Each day, two tablespoons of rice.'

Serious Drinking

I bought a brand-new drinking bowl
With money from my book.
'My Dish' is painted on the side
For those who pause to look.

I don't want any saucy mouse
To drop in for a swim.
I like to keep my water pure
And 'winking at the brim'.

Now, every dog should have a dish
As spick and span as mine,
Washed out each day and filled afresh
With Adam's sparkling wine.

And if you keep yourself topped up
With water – not with beer –
You'll be a healthy dog like me –
No salmonella here!

Pilchard Fish Cakes

Makes 25–30

3 x 425g/15oz tins pilchards in tomato sauce
450g/1lb mashed potatoes
(use more if you like potatoes!)
Salt and pepper
A little HP or Worcestershire sauce
Plain flour for shaping fish cakes

Take three large tins of pilchards in a rich tomato sauce.
Next, tip the fish out on a plate, reserve the juice, of course.
Then carefully slice down each fish and take the backbone out,
Remove the roes and give them to your dog if she's about.

Line up your largest mixing bowl and slosh in all the fish,
Break up with fork or wooden spoon and beat it round the dish.
Now add the mashed potato, which has been prepared before.
You only need about a pound – but I like rather more!

.. AND BEAT IT ROUND THE DISH

Add half the tinned tomato liquid, salt and pepper too,
Some Worcestershire or HP sauce – it's really up to you.
Then mix it well till firm and smooth and sprinkle flour like snow
On worktop or on chopping board; it binds the fish, you know.

Cover two baking sheets with foil and have them close at hand,
Now shape the mixture into cakes, *fish* cakes, you understand!
When both the trays are chock-a-block, deep freeze them overnight.
Next morning, when they're frozen stiff, then bag them up real tight.

Keep plenty in the freezer with their named and dated tags,
And when you feel like fish cakes, they are always up for grabs.
Cook them from frozen: fat or oil, a little will suffice.
The outside crisp, the centre soft, so turn them once or twice.

Eat them at once on heated plates with fresh green peas as well,
Sauce, if you like, but I prefer them served *au naturel*.

Abigail's Kedgeree

Serves 2 adults and 1 dog

1 small onion
50g/2oz butter
½ teaspoon curry powder
175g/6oz boiled long-grain rice, well drained
225g/8oz cooked, flaked smoked haddock
2 hard-boiled eggs, coarsely chopped
Salt and pepper
3 tablespoons single cream

First peel the little onion and then chop it into bits,
Melt all the butter in a pan and heat it till it spits.
Turn down the heat and sweat the onion till it's clear and gold,
Stir in the curry powder and the flavour will unfold.

Next, tip the rice into the pan, *al dente*, yes, that's right,
Then add the haddock, making sure there's not a bone in sight.
Toss in the hard-boiled eggs, shake well, until it starts to steam,
Season to taste and don't forget a generous splash of cream.

Now, heat the mixture slowly and invert it on a plate
I'll simply say, *'Bon appétit'*; I know you'll think it's great!

Fish 'n' Chips

I don't think any food outstrips
A pile of golden fish and chips,
And though they're passable at home,
It's better for a gastronome
Like me to have them when I'm out,
From shops who really have the clout,
The know-how and the expertise
And hordes of customers to please.
Frying all day and half the night
The batter always crisp and light,
The fat red-hot — a vital tip
To cook the perfect fish and chip.

I well remember, when en route
From London to the Isle of Bute,
And feeling peckish, well past noon,
While driving through the streets of Troon,
To our unqualified delight,
A fish and chip shop hove in sight.
Mummy made an unscheduled stop
And disappeared inside the shop,

14

Emerging with a bursting bag
Wrapped loosely in the local rag.
We sat together in the car,
Inhaling drifts of vinegar.
The fish we shared in partnership
And I retrieved a random chip,
Delicious! How the flavours fuse
When wrapped inside the daily news!

Abigail's Omelette Treat

Serves 1 adult or 1 small dog
(Double all the quantities for big dogs)

½ slice thick white bread
25g/1oz dripping
1 large fresh egg
Salt and pepper

I like an egg poached, boiled or fried
But this is quick to do –
My very special omelette treat
For when I'm feeling blue.

Cut half a slice of thick white bread
In tiny little bits.
Melt dripping in the omelette pan
And wait until it spits.

Tip bread into the heated fat
And while it's cooking through,
Beat up the egg and seasoning
The way you usually do.

VOILA!

The bread will soon be crisp and brown
Like croûtons for a soup.
(If you don't know what croûtons are
Then you're a nincompoop!)

Mummy says that's extremely rude:
This time, I've gone too far.
You need a dictionary in French
To see what croûtons are.

Now let's get on – where were we?
Pour the egg into the pan,
Swirling it smoothly round the bread
As quickly as you can.

When cooked you serve it round and flat
Or fold it into three.
An omelette of distinction
For discerning dogs like me.

Proper Scrambled Egg

2 fresh eggs per person
1 fresh egg per dog
1 dessertspoon milk per egg
Salt and pepper
10g/½oz butter per egg

Serve on hot buttered toast

When off my food and feeling grey
The thing that tempts me most
Is Mummy's extra special way
With scrambled egg on toast.

You think this is a piece of cake?
Then, someone tell me why
So many so-called experts make
It rubbery and dry.

A scrambled egg, *par excellence,*
Is creamy, soft and light.
To fix this *pièce de résistance*
You have to treat it right.

You need a little bowl or jug;
If Mummy cooks for me,
She sometimes commandeers my mug,
A perfect size, you see.

Into the bowl she cracks the egg
Adds milk and seasoning too.
Now pay attention here, I beg,
You may learn something new.

The secret, Mummy says, is this:
Whip lightly with a fork,
But not too much, it spoils the dish.
I watch her like a hawk!

The bread goes in the toaster here
Good timing – that's the plan.
I lend a paw and volunteer
My little frying pan.

She sets the pan on medium low
The butter melts, *tout de suite.*
She adds the eggy mixture slowly,
Turning down the heat.

She stirs it with a wooden spoon,
This is the tricky bit.
It tends to thicken far too soon,
So keep your eye on it.

It's nearly done – don't leave your post –
Remove it from the heat.
Pile neatly on the buttered toast
Sit back, relax – and eat!

Spaghetti alla Cavalieri

Serves 4 – and 1 small dog

450g/1lb spaghetti cooked *al dente* 12-15 minutes
Small knob of butter to swirl over spaghetti
when cooked and drained

Sauce Cavalieri

25g/1oz dripping or oil
1 large onion, thinly sliced
350g/12oz raw minced steak
225g/8oz tomatoes, peeled
50g/2oz mushrooms, chopped
1 clove garlic, finely chopped
1 bouquet garni
Slice lemon peel
2 tablespoons tomato purée
1 bay leaf
Salt and freshly ground pepper
Dash of sherry if liked
Grated Parmesan cheese

**Spaghetti always makes me think
Of *Lady and The Tramp.*
I'm told I look a bit like her,
And wasn't he a scamp!**

I don't like meatballs, by the way,
Too heavy on my chest.
I know they had them in the film,
But Cavalieri's best.

Melt dripping in a shallow pan
And add the onion too.
Leave it for several minutes
Till it's clear and cooked right through.

Stir in the lovely lean minced steak –
It's sacrilege, I feel.
Now add tomatoes, mushrooms, garlic,
Herbs and lemon peel.

Swirl the tomato purée round
The pan and don't forget
The bay leaf and the seasoning.
You'll like the smell, I bet!

Cover the pan and let it cook
For half an hour or more.
Remove the bay leaf and the peel –
Don't drop them on the floor.

Simmer uncovered, twenty minutes,
That should be enough,
Adding the sherry, if you like –
I can't abide the stuff.

Plonk all the cooked spaghetti
On a heated serving dish.
Pour the triumphant sauce on top,
Cheese, also, if you wish.

I savour inch by tasty inch,
And sometimes I pretend
I've found a handsome dog like Tramp
To share the other end.

Pasta e Fagioli Spanielli

Serves 6

4 tablespoons virgin olive oil
2 sticks celery, finely chopped
100g/4oz prosciutto or streaky bacon, cut in small cubes
2 medium potatoes, cut in small cubes
1 red chilli pepper, finely chopped
2 cloves garlic, finely chopped
1 x 400g/14oz can peeled Italian plum tomatoes, squashed
2 x 25g/15oz cans unsalted borlotti beans, drained
1 litre/2 pints chicken or beef stock
100g/4oz short-cut macaroni
Pinch dried basil or 4 fresh basil leaves
Salt and freshly ground pepper

Now and then, Daddy makes this spectacular soup
Though it's certainly not meant for me.
But it's simply delicious
And highly nutritious.
I hang around waiting to see

If there might be some spillages dropped on the floor
When he's testing for taste with a spoon.
If I find a small splash
It is gone in a flash.
I collapse, breathing fire, in a swoon.

Heat the oil in a very large saucepan; when hot
Add the celery, ham – that smells nice –
Plus the spuds and the chilli –
No, don't be so silly –
That doesn't mean 'cold', it's a spice!

Cook this gently, on low, for ten minutes or so
With the garlic, and don't let it stick.
Next, tomatoes, well bashed
In a bowl till they're mashed,
Then it's into the pan double-quick.

After ten minutes more add two-thirds of the beans
With the stock: turn the heat up and boil.
Add the pasta at last,
You can cook it quite fast
About ten minutes – don't let it spoil.

Now the basil goes in and the rest of the beans
Which you've smashed to a kind of a paste.
Add the pepper and salt
Call a culinary halt.
Simmer well, then it's time for a taste.

I'll be very surprised if you don't like this soup
Because Daddy's the best in the book.
In fact, Mummy told me
It's no secret that she
Only married him 'cos he could cook!

The Garden Party

Flaming June is the month for a party outdoors,
The most beautiful time of the year.
For my friends, there's much brushing and washing of paws
As they travel from far and from near.

Last year was a scorcher: I woke up at dawn
To keep tabs on the food and the drink.
We arranged trestle tables and chairs on the lawn
And kept daisy chains cool by the sink.

The morning was spent in a flurry of toil,
Boiling eggs, slicing chicken and ham.
We froze mountains of ice, so that nothing would spoil,
And made trifle with strawberry jam.

Laddie called in to pick up the charcoal and stuff
For the barbecue up in the yard.
It takes time to heat through, so it's glowing enough
To get burgers and bangers well charred!

I set bowls of iced water by flowerbed and lawn –
Asked the residents not to encroach –
Then a squeal of the brakes and the sound of a horn
Meant my friends were arriving – by coach.

What a splendid idea; take a carriage for hire,
Such a sensible way to survive.
You can paint the town red, set the river on fire,
And there's no need to drink and to drive.

I started them off with the egg-and-spoon race
'Cos we needed the eggs for our lunch.
They all charged down the lawn at a rattling good pace
With Samantha the best of the bunch.

Laddie called from the yard that the burgers were grilled
And the sausages done to a T.
There was quite a stampede for the plates to be filled,
Then they squeezed round the table with me.

As the sun filtered down through the old willow tree,
I examined the prospect with pride.
Plates of ham, eggs and chicken, fish pâté and Brie
And the daisies festooned round the side.

Conversation was nil till we burst at the seams
And dessert was – pro tem – out of court.
So we lay in the shade dreaming wonderful dreams
And I read from my book, *Paws for Thought*.

With our vigour restored, we repaired to the field
To play rounders, by mutual request.
I selected the teams, keeping talents concealed,
King Charles Spaniels, of course, v. The Rest.

Oscar collared the bat 'cos he's frightfully keen,
And Prince Rupert bowled first, pulling rank.
Oscar got to first base as he swiped it between
Woodstock Rousseau and Charlie, the Yank.

Next came Bonnie who chalked up a fabulous score
As did Paddington, Henry and Bert.
Port and Starboard and Tink added seventeen more
And, surprisingly, no one got hurt!

It was Cavaliers next and our batsmen were great,
Striking out with a lethal top spin.
With me, Meggie and Christobel, Sophie and Kate
It was never in doubt we could win.

We declared it a draw when we'd all had enough
And strolled back to the garden for tea.
There was trifle and fruit cup and best chocolate fluff
Which is always a favourite with me.

32

When we'd eaten our fill, I revealed my surprise –
A great pop group, renowned for their din,
Were engaged for the evening: five regular guys
Had arrived in the barn and plugged in.

They were known as The Scoundrels, quite famous, I'm told,
And they certainly played with panache.
We were all on cloud nine as we rocked and we rolled
And the evening went by in a flash.

There was all kinds of dancing: the vicar unbent
And obliged with a neat buck and wing.
Bobbie asked me to dance – he's not much of a gent,
But of booksellers, absolute king!

At a quarter to twelve we sang 'God Save The Queen',
For the coach had arrived in the lane.
They all said what a wonderful day it had been
And they hoped I would ask them again.

I remained in the road, waving hard till they went
From my sight: then I stood by the door
Gazing up at the stars, with a sigh of content,
As the silence swirled round me once more.

Best Chocolate Fluff

Serves 6 people – and 1 small dog

1 sachet (11g/½oz approx.) gelatine
100g/4oz good plain chocolate
4 dessertspoons milk
1 large tin evaporated milk,
chilled for 24 hours
2 dessertspoons caster sugar
A little grated chocolate for decoration

Note: after adding the chocolate, don't beat too much or the pudding will sink!

There are those who think dogs don't like puddings at all.
Well, just try us, you'll find that we do.
This is only for special occasions, of course,
But it might be of interest to you.

Sprinkle gelatine over a cup that's half full
Of cold water – and place in a pan
With two inches of water, stir, turn up the heat
And dissolve it, as smooth as you can.

Put the cup on one side till the liquid is cool,
Meanwhile, break up the chocolate in squares
In a bowl with the milk, over heat, till it looks
Like the chocolate on chocolate eclairs.

Take the bowl from the pan, stirring well while it cools.
Have your big mixing bowl by your paw.
Add the tinned milk and sugar and whisk it round fast
Till there's twice as much there as before.

Pour the gelatine in, when it's cool and beat well.
Fold the chocolate in gently, by spoon.
Whisk with care till it's blended, turn into a dish.
Lick the bowl – you'll be over the moon!

Keep the fluff in the fridge till you're ready to eat.
Dress it up with some fresh chocolate flakes.
Serve with cream, if you're eager to push out the boat –
Here's a pudding that's got what it takes!

Liver Casserole

Serves 5 – and 1 small dog

Dripping
2 medium onions, sliced
12 slices pig's liver, washed and dried
Seasoned plain flour to coat
1.35 litres/1½ pints of liquid;
(from stock cubes, or any left-over gravy)
1 clove garlic, crushed
Seasoning
8 carrots, scraped and sliced lengthwise
8 rashers streaky bacon

To cook
Have ready a large casserole and
cook at gas mark 6/400°F/200°C for 30 minutes.
After adding carrots and bacon,
simmer at gas mark 3/325°F/170°C for 30-45 minutes.

One thing I have occasionally – I just adore the smell –
Is Mummy's liver casserole, a dish she does quite well.
Some people don't like liver, in fact, Daddy's not too keen,
But when she makes this casserole, his plate is sparkling clean.
Bring out your biggest frying pan, the one that's hard to lift.
Fry onions in the heated fat. And don't forget to sift
The flour to coat the liver, making sure it's smooth and thick
Then drop the meat into the pan and watch it doesn't stick.

Now, should the onions start to catch, transfer them to a dish
Or put them in the casserole to settle if you wish.
When both sides of the liver are a tasty shade of brown
Transfer it to the casserole and turn the heat right down
Beneath the heavy frying pan: remove the surplus fat,
Then add the melted stock cubes or the gravy, and when that
Is hot, take up your wooden spoon and, quickly as you can,
Scrape up all those delicious bits found sticking to the pan.
Next, sprinkle in the garlic, boil it up and stir it well
Now pour into the casserole and revel in the smell!
Check seasoning, put on the lid, make sure the oven's hot,
And bake the dish for half an hour, remove it on the dot.

Add, in neat rows, the carrots and the streaky bacon too.
Return to cooler oven and that's all you have to do.
Oh, no it's not! I quite forgot: wait till it's cooked right through,
Turn up the grill to blazing hot. The last thing you must do
Is take the lid off; place the dish beneath the searing heat
And when the bacon frizzles up at last it's time to eat!

Lamb Chops

My nose is quick to tell me when lamb chops are on display;
I stay on guard beside the stove to speed them on their way.
I know how to prepare them, I'm a connoisseur, by Jove –
The first thing is to rub them with a big, fat garlic clove.

Leave till the flavour is absorbed, then activate the grill.
When glowing red, slide in the pan and move in for the kill.
The chops will soon be crispy, but before they start to catch,
Flip over with the tongs and cook the other side to match.

When nearly done, lift out the pan and – generous to a fault –
Give them a hearty sprinkle with your favourite seasoned salt.
Return them to the grill, each side will need a minute more,
By which time all the family will be waiting – such a bore.

There's never one left over and I think it's very mean.
It wouldn't hurt to cut me off a tiny bit of lean.
Chop bones for dogs are not allowed, but Daddy is my friend;
He lets me have a nibble while he holds the other end.

BE WARNED – and do not emulate my bony expertise –
It isn't safe for little dogs, so don't attempt it, please!

Sausages

Oh, isn't a sausage a wonderful thing
When it's crispy and shiny and brown?
Not at all like those objects that hang on a string
In the butcher's shop window in town.

The sausage fills many a talented role
From the merely mundane to the flash.
You can bake it in batter as toad-in-the-hole,
Or go easy with bangers and mash.

You can buy them with herbs, and organically stuffed,
Or surrounded by beans in a tin.
At the delicatessen I'm soundly rebuffed
When I stand at the door and peep in.

For the tempting aroma that hangs in the air,
Liver sausage, salami and pork
Are as much as a literary gourmet can bear
When she's tired from her work and her walk.

There are frankfurter sausages, pickled in brine,
That are heated and served in a bun.
They are known as 'hot dogs', which is way out of line
And it's not my idea of a pun.

With drinks, they have sausages served on a stick
And they often get dropped on the ground,
Which is bully for me, for I don't miss a trick
As I busily hoover around.

There are those who like sausages swimming in grease
Irrespective of culinary skill,
But if you have a dog who is slightly obese
You should sizzle them under the grill.

Steak and Kidney Pie

Serves 6

1.25kg/2½lb chuck steak, cubed
175g/6oz kidney, chopped small
Plain flour to coat
2 medium onions, sliced
Dripping
1.35 litres/1½ pints beef stock
or equivalent gravy, enough to cover meat
Salt and pepper
225g/8oz rich shortcrust pastry,
chill in fridge till required
Beaten egg for glaze

To cook
Brush with beaten egg, snip 4 air holes with scissors.
Preheat oven to gas mark 7/425°F/220°C and cook for 10 minutes.
Lower heat to gas mark 4/350°F/180°C and cook for 25-30 minutes.

I always keep my station when it's steak and kidney pie,
I sit beneath the chopping board and watch the pieces fly.
Occasionally she drops a bit: I think it's by design,
Well, maybe it's by accident, but anyhow it's mine.

The meat is tossed in plain white flour, but what I like the most
Is when she fries the onion strips in dripping from the roast.
My nose is working overtime, as only noses can,
The meat, like little snowballs now, is added to the pan.

The next thing is the liquid and, a most important point,
She either uses stock cubes or some gravy from the joint.
She stirs it with a wooden spoon and soon it starts to cook,
Down goes the heat, bang goes the lid – I'm not allowed to look.

She sometimes adds the seasoning now and sometimes later on,
And lets it simmer slowly till about two hours have gone.
When cool, it fills my favourite dish, Italian, blue and white
It stands there in the kitchen and it haunts me all the night.

Next day, she takes the pastry from the fridge and rolls it out,
Skims off the fat that tops the meat. (She knows what she's about!)
She makes a cover for the pie as neatly as can be,
Then adds a little pastry dog which sort of looks like me.

When everything is ready and they open up the pie
I have to sit and watch them, it's enough to make you cry.
There's never much left over but I once licked out the dish,
And truth to tell, I have to say, it's just as good as fish!

Christmas Turkey

We always have turkey at Christmas
And sometimes at Easter, with luck.
It will last us for days
Served in various ways,
And it's bigger than chicken or duck!

We pack it up front with the stuffing,
And the sausagemeat goes at the stern.
Then we sprinkle it well
With *du poivre et du sel.*
(That's my French; I've just started to learn.)

Next, massage the turkey with onion,
Brush with butter, or oil if preferred.
Now, I'll give you a tip
That an expert let slip,
Sift ground ginger all over the bird.

You may think the idea is crazy,
I can sense your superior grin,
But you'll find when you baste,
There's no smell and no taste
And it gives it a fabulous skin.

I sometimes assist with the bacon
Strips of streaky to cover the breast,
Which leaves Mummy on course
To prepare the bread sauce,
Chipolatas and sprouts and the rest.

We tuck lots of foil round the turkey
And it seems to take ages to cook,
So I have a quick snooze,
Give an ear to my muse
And compose a few lines for my book.

At forty-five minutes to blast-off,
We open the big oven door.
When the foil is unrolled,
It still hasn't turned gold,
So we leave it to swelter some more.

When Mummy has doctored the gravy
And the turkey is ready to scoff,
Then I take up my stand,
Where the pickings will land,
Daddy sharpens his knife and we're off!

Fine favours descend from the carver,
Crispy skin, which I simply adore,
Scraps of bacon and breast
And, if I'm at my best,
There's no chance of it reaching the floor.

To roast an exceptional chicken,
You can copy the things we've done here.
I must go: I've been told
Christmas lunch is on hold,
So I'll wish you a Happy New Year.

Turkey Soup

1 turkey carcass
6 carrots
6 potatoes
3 onions
Dripping
Water to cover carcass
Salt and pepper

Serve with French bread

You can make lovely soup from a turkey.
I'm not keen but it seems *de rigueur.*
When you've had it cold, twice,
And *réchauffé* with rice
It's kaput for a cool connoisseur.

Firstly, line up two carrots, one onion,
And the carcass stripped bare as can be.
You can toss the whole bunch
In a pan after lunch,
And allow it to simmer till tea.

You should scoop off the scum when it's boiling
Put the lid on and let well alone.
When it's done, strain the broth
Through a sieve or a cloth,
Getting rid of the debris and bone.

Sweat an onion or two in some dripping;
Add potatoes and carrots, *tout de suite.*
Cook, with some of the stock,
In your pan or your wok
And stand by till it's ready to eat.

No! Don't eat it. We haven't quite finished.
Tip it into the blender and pour
All the stock on the top
Whizz it round and then stop,
Start it up and rotate it some more.

Next, tip it back into the saucepan,
Heat it through, put the seasoning right.
Warm the bread and the plates
Then assemble your mates –
Pour it out, drink it up and goodnight.

Chez Moi

When leaves have almost vanished from the garden,
And daylight disappears at half-past three,
Then we've crossed the Rubicon
And my thinking cap goes on
For it's time to plan my annual jamboree.

I always give a party in the winter
To entertain my closest friends *chez moi.*
It's a popular event,
Invitations must be sent
For my soirées have that chic *je ne sais quoi.*

There's milk shakes, egg flip, beer and Bovril cocktails:
Dogs rarely touch an alcoholic drink.
Though, last year, a friend of mine
Brought a case of home-made wine.
It was horrid and we poured it down the sink.

I have some help from Mummy with the punch bowl.
She chops up lots of fruit to make it nice.
Then we add the H_2O
From a highland spring we know
And I top it up with cubes of sparkling ice.

The 'eats', of course, are my especial forte
I'm famous for my canapés and dips.
But my female friends confess
That too much of my largesse
Spells disaster and a lifetime on the hips!

Last year we had a special celebration,
When *Paws Again* was published in the fall.
All my friends came by to look
And to buy my latest book,
Then they crowded round for cocktails in the hall.

Prince Rupert was the first, he brought me roses.
He doffed his hat, bowed low and kissed my paw.
Then the London lot swarmed in
Simply bursting to begin
And my other guests soon hurtled through the door.

The canapés were handed round by Laddie.
He always helps and knows just what to do.
Chipolatas speared with sticks,
A delicious tuna mix
And my own amazing liver pâté too.

I have to say, *les deux pièces de résistance*
Were piquant shortbread biscuits, ooh la la!
And the wafers, crisp and cheesy –
Both these recipes are easy
And they certainly knock spots off caviare.

Young Woodstock Rousseau stuffed himself with Twiglets
And Henry found the beer: I'll say no more.
Then that rowdy London bunch
Dropped the peanuts in the punch
And wee Oscar had to fish them out by paw.

When things were getting mildly out of order
We heard a fracas going on outside.
It was Sapphire – always late –
With a limo at the gate.
She had lost her way and had to hitch a ride.

Prince Rupert filled her goblet from the punch bowl
And Sapphire tossed her head and flashed her eyes.
I observed this tête-à-tête
And was pleased that they had met
But I felt a stab of pain – to my surprise.

By this time there was dancing in the parlour,
And Christobel stepped out with Charlie Two.
Port and Starboard did the tango,
Busby cut a mean fandango
Clasping Emma, who had clearly downed a few.

Prince Rupert really hit it off with Sapphire
And walked her in the garden for a while.
It was plain for all to see
That he'd given up on me
Since I failed to make the journey down the aisle.

I sat down on the stairs with Bert and Meggie
And Paddington, not long returned from France.
He's been living there for years,
So my French offends his ears,
But he lost no time in asking me to dance.

Soon everyone was feeling rather sleepy.
The food was gone, the punch bowl very low.
Crowding round to shake my paw,
They made tracks towards the door.
It was late but I was sad to see them go.

I hoovered up the crumbs and cleared the glasses,
And Laddie stayed to help me put things straight.
We enjoyed a final drink
As I polished up the sink,
Then I said goodnight and saw him to the gate.

Prince Rupert's hat was lying in the garden.
I picked it up and carried it inside.
I would keep it to remind me
Of the joys I left behind me,
In the days when Rupert hoped I'd be his bride.

I curled up on my beanbag – quite exhausted –
Reviewing my undoubted *tour de force*.
It will not remain unnoticed
I'm the hostess with the mostest
And I'll do it all again next year – of course!

Abigail's Amazing Liver Pâté

Makes 25 nibbles

1 x 300g/10½oz tin undiluted beef consommé
A dash each: ground mace, cinnamon, garlic powder, thyme
1 sachet (11g/½oz approx.) gelatine, soaked in cold water
1 x 100g/4oz good liver pâté
Brandy to taste

Serve on Petit Toasts, or small crackers

Oh boy! this is good and it's terribly easy
And marvellous for serving with drinks.
All your friends will assume you've been slaving for days
And it's done in a couple of winks.

Tip the consommé into a fairly small saucepan
Then toss in the herbs – what a brew!
Bring it all to the boil, turn it down to a simmer
And leave for a minute or two.

Stir the gelatine into the consommé mixture,
Then into the blender it goes.
Add the pâté and blend at top speed for ten seconds,
No more, so please stay on your toes.

Add a generous dash of your very best brandy
(The one that you keep for the vet!),
Pour it into a mould, which you've rinsed in cold water,
And leave in the fridge till it's set.

You can spread it on crackers or very small toasts
And you'll find that it's always a wow.
If your friends want the recipe, show them my book
Then they'll go out and buy it – right now!

Piquant Shortbread Biscuits

Makes 2 oven trays full

275g/10oz plain flour
½ teaspoon salt
¼ teaspoon dry mustard
¼ teaspoon cayenne pepper
275g/10oz margarine
275g/10oz finely grated cheese

Filling
100g/4oz butter
1 teaspoon Marmite

To cook
Line oven trays with Bakewell paper.
Cook in preheated oven gas mark 5/375°F/190°C.

You don't have to make such enormous amounts
But it's quite a good plan: well, just think –
They will freeze! Then you've always got something on hand
If a friend should drop in for a drink.

Sieve the flour and the seasonings into a bowl.
Cream the marg in the mixer and then
Add the cheese; dry ingredients; switch on once more,
They will bind while you count up to ten.

Take the dough from the mixer and knead into rolls,
Like bananas, six ounces in weight.
Put them into the fridge for one hour to cool off,
Or deep freeze, with the name and the date.

To cook: cut into rounds of a quarter-inch thick
And arrange on a paper-lined tray.
Bake in preheated oven, as set out above,
For about fifteen minutes, I'd say.

Let them cool on a rack while you mix up the filling,
Then sandwich together in pairs.
If you're swarming with guests, take a leaf out of my book
And stash a few under the stairs!

Crispy Cheese Wafers

The quantities will depend on how many you want to make.

2 (or more) packets of ice-cream wafers
Melted butter
Hard Cheddar cheese, *finely* grated (to coat wafers)

Pastry brush
Greaseproof paper for tossing cheese round the wafers

To cook
Cook in preheated oven gas mark 5/375°F/190°C for about
7 minutes.
Eat the same day or store in airtight tin.

Cut the packets of wafers in half so they're square
And annoint with a butter-soaked brush.
Coat them well with the cheese, which you've grated with care,
Line them up on a tray (and don't rush
To inform all your friends of this singular treat) –
Let them cook in the oven till done.
When they're crisp, take them out, cool them off and discreetly
Half-inch one or two, just for fun!

If you like to have something unique up your sleeve
Keep this recipe under your hat.
It's a sure-fire success and I firmly believe
No one knows it but me, so that's that!

Tuna Dip

100g/4oz tin tuna fish, drained
300ml/½ pint sour cream
225g/8oz cream cheese
1 clove garlic, minced
Dash of tabasco
A little salt

This is useful for breaking the ice.
Guests can all help themselves, which is nice.
There is nothing to cook,
Which is one for the book,
And I've made it myself, once or twice.

Put the fish and the cream and the cheese
In the blender and mix by degrees
With the garlic; a touch
Of tabasco – not much –
Add the salt. *C'est fini* – it's a breeze!